THE WITCH'S HAT

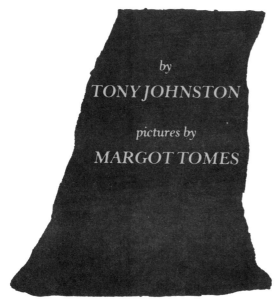

by
TONY JOHNSTON

pictures by
MARGOT TOMES

A BANTAM LITTLE ROOSTER BOOK

NEW YORK · TORONTO · LONDON · SYDNEY · AUCKLAND

THE WITCH'S HAT

A BANTAM LITTLE ROOSTER BOOK / PUBLISHED BY ARRANGEMENT
WITH G.P. PUTNAM'S SONS

PRINTING HISTORY
G.P. Putnam's Sons edition published 1984
Bantam edition / October 1991

ISBN 0-553-35354-3

Published simultaneously in the United States and Canada

PRINTED IN THE UNITED STATES OF AMERICA

LBM   0 9 8 7 6 5 4 3 2 1

For Ashley, my porkus,

my hamus, in pink pajamas −TJ

For Frith, the cat −MT

A witch was stirring her brew in a big, fat, magic pot.

She stirred and stirred.

Then she bent to taste, and — oops — her hat fell in.
"My hat!" she screeched in a voice as thin as she was.
"I'll have to fish it out."

She fished

and fished.

Then, when she felt a nibble, she pulled up the soggy hat.

"My hat!" she cackled happily.

But when she reached for it—the hat turned into a bat.

(It was a magic pot, in case you forgot.)

"My hat is a bat!" cried the witch. "Hat! Stop, I say!"
But did it stop?

No. It flew away.

It settled in the attic.

The attic was dark. Was the witch brave?

Would she go inside? Yes.

She squinted. And what did she see?

A whole flock of bats hanging from a rafter.

"Oh, fine," she grumbled. "Which one is mine?"

She called out, "Hat, come down!"

Nothing moved. Not one bat. Not one hat.

"Grrrrrrrr," said the witch, grinding her teeth. She mumbled a magic spell, "Porkus, hamus, pink pajamas," and — *all* the bats fluttered down and piled around her knees.

"Which one are you?" asked the witch in a grouchy voice. Did anyone answer?

No. Not one bat. Not one hat.

So she began to pinch the bats to find her very own.

"Squeak!" went a bat.

"Bat," said the witch.

"Squeak!" went a bat.
"Bat," said the witch.

"Ouch!" went a bat.
"HAT!" cried the witch.
She grabbed for it, but—

it turned into a rat.

(It was a magic pot, in case you forgot.)

"My hat is a rat! Stop, I say!"

But did it stop?

No. It scrambled into a hole in the wall.

The hole was dark.

Was the witch brave? Yes.

Would she go inside? No. She wouldn't fit.

"We'll see about that, hat," muttered the witch.

She fetched a cheese, big as you please, and —

a whole river of rats poured
from the hole and began to
gnaw that cheese.

The witch began to poke the rats to find her very own.

"Oooh," went a rat. "Rat," said the witch.

"Oooh," went a rat.

"Rat," said the witch.

"Boo!" went a rat.

"HAT!" cried the witch.

She grabbed for it, but—

now it wasn't a rat. Now it was a cat.

(It was a magic pot, in case you forgot.)

The cat ran downstairs
like an inky streak.

The witch ran after it.
But when she reached
the last stair, what was there?

Twenty-seven cats from who-knows-where,

purring on the hearth.

The witch wasn't purring. She was roaring.

"I'm going to get you, hat!"

She tickled the cats to find her very own.

"Meow," went a cat. "Cat," said the witch.

"Meow," went a cat.
"Cat," said the witch.

"Tee-hee-hee," went a cat.
"HAT!" cried the witch,
pouncing on it with both hands
and popping it on her head.

The witch went back to stir her brew.
All was well. She had her very own hat.

She was smiling now. And—

the magic pot was smiling too.